Dear Harriet
Happy Reading and
Sweet Dreams!
Vx.

Dear Harriet,
Merry Christmas
x
Best wishes,
Daniel

Daniel Craig
Vicky x

For Tom.

At last the girls got their small baby brother!

In the depths of the forest a baby was born,
A beautiful Deer gave birth to a fawn,
He had huge dark brown eyes, with long thick black lashes,
And the shiniest fur, with little white splashes.
His father stood tall and announced at his side,
"I welcome my son with much love and great pride."

His thin bandy legs, they wobbled and shook,
And the whole of the family were desperate to look
At this curious boy, with their wonderful mother,
At last not a girl, but a small baby BROTHER!

The sisters were squawking "Oh isn't he sweet!
But the small boy can barely stand up on his feet!"

"Oh dearest Deer, do not judge at first glance,
He'll grow strong in good time, if you give him a chance."

The fawn did grow quickly, but there was a hitch,
Between his small ears he'd developed an itch.
He'd tried scratching his itch with his own little foot,
But it just didn't work and the itch had stayed put.

"Oh Mother Deer!" he said with a screech,
"I've got a tickle that I just can't reach."

"Oh dear my Deer, that just won't do,
Come right next to me and I'll scratch it for you.
A nuisance tickle? We don't like those."
And she rubbed his small head with her velvety nose.

The young fawn grew stocky, the young fawn grew fine,
And his wobbly legs grew in strength all the time.
Alas, it was not just the young fawn that grew,
The bigger HE got, his tickles got TOO!!

He tried having a scratch on an old piece of wood,
But it just didn't work, it was doing no good.

Just then, with a cackle and flap of a feather,
Wise Graham the Grouse popped out of the heather.

"Hello dear boy, how are you?" he said,
"I hear you've a tickle on top of your head."

"Oh Graham I have and it's been there all day,
It's behind my right ear and it won't go away.
Please can you help me as you are so wise,
What should I try next? What would you advise?"

"Oh dear my Deer, I have no idea,
Why you have a tickle behind your right ear,
You see I don't have fur, but a mass of fine feathers,
To allow me to fly, and stay warm in foul weathers.
I'm sorry to hear of this problem of yours."
And with that he flew off, across the wild moors.

The fawn grew quite big, the fawn grew so strong,
And the splashes of white in his smooth coat were gone,
But although he got bigger and stronger each day,
His tickly tickles would not go away.

He tried having an itch on an old piece of fence,
But it just didn't work, and it didn't make sense.
And just when he thought that he couldn't get madder,
He heard the sly hissing of Alan the Adder.

"Greetings my dear," Alan spat with a smile,
"Have you still got those tickles you've had for a while?"

"I certainly do, and they won't disappear,
It tickles like crazy behind my left ear."

"Oh dear my Deer, I do find it queer,
That you have a tickle behind your left ear.
You're a hairy thing… if you want my advice,
I think that you're probably crawling with lice.
I don't want to bore you with minor details,
But you don't get these problems when covered in scales."

With a venomous glance, and his most hostile smile,
Off slid Alan the Adder, the most vile of reptiles.

The big fawn grew brave, the big fawn grew clever,
But his tickly tickles felt stronger than ever.

"I must have a scratch, I can't take anymore,
My tickles are prickles and really quite sore!"

He tried having a rub on a rock in the gill,
But it just didn't work, and the itch was there STILL!

He felt so frustrated he started to weep,
And his snuffles were heard by old Shirley the Sheep.

"Good evening my dear, now come dry those tears,
Have you still got those tickles around your big ears?"

"Oh Shirley I have and they're driving me mad,
I'm sorry you've spotted me feeling so sad."

"Oh my dear Deer, I HAVE AN IDEA,
Why you have these tickles around your big ears,
We sheep aren't renowned for being the brightest,
But please listen to me and don't fret in the slightest."

"Now I don't have fur, I have thick wool that's curly,
But I'd ask your Father," said knowing old Shirley.
"Your Father should know about tickles I think."
And with that she left, and she gave him a wink.

The fawn's heart filled with hope, and so did his head,
So he dashed to find Father as Shirley had said.

"Oh Daddy Deer! I've had such fears,
About terrible tickles around my big ears."

"Oh dear my Deer, you should have said,
That you had such tickles upon your grand head."
With a chuckle he took his son down to the loch,
To see his reflection… And WOW… what a shock!!

As the loch water cleared, the young red deer
Saw magnificent antlers begin to appear.

This publication was printed sustainably in the UK by Pureprint, a CarbonNeutral® company with FSC® chain of custody and an ISO 14001 certified environmental management system recycling over 99% of all dry waste.

Designed by GIG Retail.

ISBN 9781527283671

He was now a grand stag and his antlers were strong,
And his tickly tickles had FINALLY GONE!!